The Night Before Christmas

A Visit from St. Nicholas

by Clement C. Moore

Brown Watson
ENGLAND

'Twas the night before Christmas,
    when all through the house
Not a creature was stirring,
    not even a mouse;

The stockings were hung
        by the chimney with care,
In hopes that St. Nicholas
        soon would be there.

The children were nestled
all snug in their beds,
While visions of sugarplums
danced in their heads;

And mamma in her kerchief,
and I in my cap,
Had just settled our brains
for a long winter nap;

When out on the lawn
  there arose such a clatter,
I sprang from my bed
  to see what was the matter.

Away to the window
    I flew like a flash,
Tore open the shutters
    and threw up the sash.

The moon, on the breast
    of the new-fallen snow,
Gave a lustre of midday
    to objects below,

When, what to my wondering
eyes should appear,
But a miniature sleigh
and eight tiny reindeer,

With a little old driver
　　so lively and quick,
I knew in a moment
　　it must be St. Nick.

More rapid than eagles,
  his coursers they came,
And he whistled and shouted
  and called them by name:

"Now, Dasher! now, Dancer!
now, Prancer and Vixen!

On Comet! on Cupid!
on Donner and Blitzen!
To the top of the porch,
to the top of the wall,

Now, dash away! dash away!
dash away all!"

As dry leaves that before
the wild hurricane fly,
When they meet with an obstacle,
mount to the sky,

So up to the housetop
   the coursers they flew,
With the sleigh full of toys,
   and St. Nicholas, too.

And then, in a twinkling,
     I heard on the roof
The prancing and pawing
     of each little hoof.
As I drew in my head,
     and was turning around,
Down the chimney St. Nicholas
     came with a bound.
He was dressed all in fur
     from his head to his foot,
And his clothes were all tarnished
     with ashes and soot;

A bundle of toys
he had flung on his back,
And he looked like a pedlar
just opening his pack.

His eyes – how they twinkled!
His dimples – how merry!
His cheeks were like roses,
his nose like a cherry.

His droll little mouth
was drawn up like a bow,
And the beard on his chin
was as white as the snow.

He had a broad face
and a little round belly
That shook when he laughed
like a bowlful of jelly.

He was chubby and plump,
a right jolly old elf,
And I laughed when I saw him
in spite of myself.

A wink of his eye
and a twist of his head
Soon gave me to know
I had nothing to dread.

He spoke not a word,
    but went straight to his work,
And filled all the stockings;
    then turned with a jerk,

And laying his finger
   aside of his nose,
And giving a nod,
   up the chimney he rose.

He sprang to his sleigh,
to his team gave a whistle
And away they all flew
like the down of a thistle.